Sinbad the Pig

by Anne and Robert O'Brien
illustrated by Meg McLean

Open Court Publishing Company

Printed in the United States of America

ISBN 0-8126-1274-4

10 9

Sinbad Acts Fast

Gramps and Anna have a big pig.

4

The pig is Sinbad.
Sinbad has bad habits.

Sinbad tips Gramps.

Gramps grabs at Sinbad.
Sinbad acts fast!

7

8

Sinbad and Anna

"Grab the pig, Anna!" says Gramps.

Sinbad is fast.
He spins past Anna.

Anna grabs at Sinbad.
Gramps grins.

"I have him!" says Anna.

Sinbad sits.

Anna trips on the pig.

Anna stamps.
Gramps grins.

"Sinbad, you have bad habits!" says Anna.